KERI TARR
CAT DETECTIVE

Wendy Lement

Illustrated by Jeffrey Scott Burrows

BREAKAWAY BOOKS
HALCOTTSVILLE, NY
2004

Keri Tarr: Cat Detective
Copyright 2000, 2004 by Wendy Lement
Illustrations copyright by Jeffrey Scott Burrows

Library of Congress Control Number: 2004093400
ISBN: 1-891369-52-0
Printed in China

Published by Breakaway Books
P.O. Box 24
Halcottsville, NY 12438
(800) 548-4348
www.breakawaybooks.com

FIRST EDITION

For my niece Keri
with love

1

The birth of Mew

Sally was in a panic. She had been mewing for over an hour. Not a regular mew like when she was hungry, but the kind of clamor she only made in the car when they drove her to the vet—an unearthly wail that made the entire family feel as if they were torturing her. *They deserve to feel that way,* she always thought on those agonizing trips to the vet. After all, the traumatic car ride was followed by pinching and prodding in and around every part of her body. No place was sacred. On those occasions, Keri would hold her and pet her, and tell her how beautiful she was, which was true. Sally was an outstanding cat and she knew it.

But tonight, Sally wasn't in the car. She was alone in the basement. It was three o'clock in the morning, and the family was sound asleep two flights above. No one heard her cries for help. In truth, she wasn't completely alone, and that was the reason for her desperate calls. Just one hour earlier, Sally did something she had never done before, something she didn't know she could do. Sally had given birth to a tiny black kitten with white markings. Without thinking, she had licked and cleaned it. Now the black ball of fur—no bigger than the

5

mouse she had caught and played with two days before—lay fast asleep, nestled beside her.

Sally was not just proud of her achievement, she was ecstatic. That was the reason for all the racket. The birth itself had been painless. But Sally had accomplished an amazing feat, and she wanted to show off, especially to Keri, who was her best friend. "What to do?" she fretted. All that mewing had exhausted her, and still no one stirred. She couldn't bear the thought of leaving her offspring alone while she made the trip upstairs. No, there was only one solution.

Sally wrapped her mouth tightly around the back of her kitten's neck and began the long trek up the basement stairs. She made her way through the kitchen and into the living room, where she carefully dropped the baby cat onto the soft blue carpet so they both could rest. "Just one more flight," Sally moaned as she licked her kitten. But the second flight took even longer. Sally was unusually small for an adult cat, and she felt weak from the ordeal. Once she made it, she knew Keri would hold her and kiss her, and tell her how special she was.

Sally turned right at the top of the stairs into Keri's room and gently placed her kitten in the center of the round cotton rug that lay beside Keri's bed. It took every bit of strength that Sally could muster, but she jumped up onto the bed with one not-so-graceful leap. This was serious business, so she skipped the ritual nudging at Keri's arm and licking of her toes, and went straight for her head. "Mew, mew, mew," she cried as she crawled back and forth through Keri's black hair.

"Cut it out," Keri complained, still half asleep. But Sally

persisted. "Stop it!" Keri ordered, but Sally only mewed louder and jumped full force back on her head.

This battle continued for several minutes until Sally, exasperated, performed her second miraculous act of the evening. In a raspy voice, she pleaded, "Keri, wake up. You have to see what I did!" At this, Keri opened one eye. *I must be dreaming,* she thought as her head fell back on the pillow.

"Please Keri. This is urgent!"

"Mom?" Keri whispered, opening both her eyes wide.

"It's me, Sally. Would ya get up already?"

Keri did get up. In fact, she bolted to the light switch on the wall, almost crushing Sally's kitten beneath her feet.

"Careful, you idiot!" Sally shouted.

"I'm not an idiot." Keri switched on the light and surveyed the room, but to her surprise, no one was there. "Mom!"

"It's me! Me!" Sally insisted. Keri stared at her up-till-now ordinary black cat. "Now can I show you what I did?"

"Sally?" Keri replied, still convinced she must be dreaming.

"Yeah, it's me, Sally. I've been trying to wake you up forever. Look at this." She jumped off the bed onto the rug. Keri took a step toward her. "Careful!" Sally hissed.

"What?"

"You'll step on him."

"Who?"

"Look!"

Now, for the first time, Keri noticed the tiny black ball in the center of her rug. "Did you kill another mouse?"

Insulted, Sally picked up her kitten and started toward the door. "A mouse," she muttered. "She thinks it's a mouse."

"Wait." Keri inspected the black squirming object dangling from Sally's mouth. Her eyes grew even wider. "It's a kitten."

"You think I'd give birth to an orangutan? Of course it's a kitten."

"But how? When? What happened?" Keri asked a thousand questions, to which Sally gave long, mostly exaggerated answers. The birth took hours. She thought she would die. Every detail was embellished—the long trip up the stairs, thinking each step would be her last.

Keri listened intently as if it were perfectly natural to be conversing with a cat. "Then what happened?" "Oh you poor thing." And so on. For the next hour and a half they sat on the rug, poring over the evening's events. "What's his name?" Keri finally asked.

"Mew."

"No, I mean in English."

"I told you: Mew. It's the same in Human and in Cat."

"Mew." Keri laughed. And so it was.

2

The Tarrs

On Saturday mornings, Keri and her older brother Dan sat on the family room floor and watched cartoons while Mom and Dad slept late. Sally curled up on Keri's lap and purred. It was her favorite time of the week—two hours of uninterrupted petting. After breakfast, Keri practiced her new saxophone while Dan played the piano. Like most cats, Sally loved music, and she'd mew along to whatever tune Keri played. There was something about the music that made her forget whatever she was doing, even forget if she was hungry—like a magic spell.

In the afternoons, Dan was too busy to play with Keri. He was always writing some screenplay for a future *Star Wars* type movie or building an intricate model of some ancient tomb for his sixth-grade class. Mom had a thousand errands to run, and Dad spent hours in the basement working on his gigantic train set, which filled an entire room. Keri didn't mind being on her own. In fact, she loved leading Sally on explorations of the woods behind their house. Keri noticed how the forest changed from week to week. In the winter, she followed animal tracks left in the snow and figured out which creature left which tracks. In the summer, while Sally chased mice, squirrels, and anything else that moved, Keri climbed trees and investigated the comings and goings of the forest's inhabitants—the ones that Sally hadn't chased away.

Sometimes they walked clear to the other side of the forest to the Bolton Public Library. The building was made of stone, which gave it the appearance of a small cave. Miss Owen, the librarian, was extremely nice. Not only did she help Keri find the best detective stories, which Keri loved, but she also let Sally roam through the stacks and stacks of books. When Sally tired of rambling over shelves, she would sit on a table and watch Keri read. She studied Keri's pretty round face, framed by

straight dark hair that fell to her shoulders and bangs that hung just above her bright brown eyes. Sally noticed that Keri's eyes widened whenever she read an exciting passage, and sparkled when she read something funny. Sometimes Keri even laughed out loud, but Miss Owen didn't mind. Keri laughed a lot, which is probably why her eyes were so bright.

On this particular Saturday morning, Keri ran through the house waking up Dan and Mom and Dad. She had planned to let her parents sleep until seven o'clock, but she was too excited. So at five twenty A.M., the family rolled out of bed and slowly made their way downstairs to the kitchen, wondering what in the world Keri was going on about. "Coffee," muttered her mom as she felt her way over to the counter.

"Okay," Keri ordered, "everyone close your eyes." This was easy. Their eyes were half closed already. "Now you can open them." Keri held out the tiny black kitten for inspection.

"It's a kitten," said Dad, wiping the sleep from his eyes.

"Where did you find it?" asked Mom. "It's too little to be a stray."

Sally interrupted: "Hello. It was me. I did that."

But only Keri understood what Sally said. The rest of the family ignored her mewing and focused all their attention on the black ball of fur in Keri's hands. "It's Sally's baby," Keri informed them. "She gave birth last night." Keri carefully placed Mew next to his proud mother.

"I didn't even know she was pregnant," Dad said with a chuckle.

"What? Did you think I was just fat?" Offended, Sally

picked up Mew and huffed out of the kitchen.

"Dad, you hurt her feelings," Keri explained.

"Oh, sorry, Sally," Dad called after her, not believing that he had done anything of the kind.

As the family munched on various flavors of cereal, Keri recounted the events of the previous evening. "And Sally said it was so painful, she almost died."

"Cats don't feel pain when they give birth. Do they, Mom?" asked Dan.

"She said she did!"

"She *said?*"

"She told me the whole thing."

"Okay, Keri," Dad said calmly, as he and Mom exchanged glances.

Keri burst into tears. In fact, she was so upset that she couldn't get another word out for over five minutes. "You don't believe me," she finally sniffled. It was true. They didn't believe her. But they were puzzled. Keri had a terrific imagination, but she wasn't a liar. She was nine years old, and that was old enough to distinguish between what was real and what was imagined.

Maybe we should take her to see Dr. Shaffer, Mom thought. Just then, Sally sulked back into the room and jumped on Keri's lap.

"Hey, where's the kitten?" Dan asked. For the next forty-five minutes the family searched the house high and low, under beds, in the basement, under the sink. Mew had disappeared. Unsuccessful, they reassembled in the kitchen to discuss what to do next.

"Why doesn't Keri ask Sally where her kitten is?" Dan joked.

"That's a great idea!" Keri rushed over to her cat. "Sally, where did you put Mew?"

"Mew?" Dan chuckled.

"That's his name!"

"Okay, Keri, Mew is a good name."

"Where's Mew?" Keri asked again.

"I don't remember," Sally answered nonchalantly.

"You do too."

Mom gently put her hand on Keri's shoulder. "Sweetie . . ."

"No, Mom, she remembers. She's just not telling me." Keri tickled Sally behind the ear. "Please tell me."

"I brought him someplace safe."

"We won't bother him. We promise. We just want to make sure he's okay."

"Well, if you must know, he's sleeping in the linen closet."

"The linen closet!" Keri announced. The family paused for a second and then raced upstairs to check. The door to the closet was open slightly. "Shhh," Keri whispered. "I promised we wouldn't disturb Mew." Slowly she opened the door, and to the family's astonishment (except of course for Keri), Mew was nestled on a pillowcase that had fallen on the closet floor. "See," Keri said very softly.

"She must have known the kitten was there before," Dan suggested.

"Did not!"

"Then ask Sally something else."

"Like what?"

"How about . . . where the blue mouse is."

"What blue mouse?"

"The one we gave her for Christmas."

"Dan," Mom protested.

"Fine. The blue mouse." Keri marched downstairs, her family trailing behind her. "Sally?"

"What now? Can't a new mother get any rest?"

"Where did you hide the mouse?"

"Which mouse?" Sally sighed, tired of the game.

"The blue one we gave you for Christmas."

"I don't know. It was dead when I got it. What's for breakfast?"

"You can eat later. I need to know."

"Eat later?!"

"Would someone fill Sally's bowl?" With this, Keri looked up at her family, who had heard nothing from Sally except the usual mews and meows of hunger.

"I'll get the cat food," Dad volunteered.

"Now will you tell me where you hid the mouse?"

"I may have left it under the cushion," Sally yawned.

"Which cushion?" There were probably fifty cushions of one kind or another in the house.

"The one on the love seat. Where's my food?"

"The love seat!" Keri shouted as she dashed to the living room, her entourage in tow. Throwing the cushions off the small sofa, Keri quickly held up a rather damaged looking bluish mouse. "Now do you believe me?"

"Yeah, I guess," conceded Dan. "But it's kind of weird."

3

Keri Tarr:
Cat Detective

For the rest of the summer, Keri and Sally held long con-
versations at night, after the rest of the family had gone to
sleep. Sally filled Keri in on all the news she heard from other
cats in the neighborhood who came to the back porch to visit
her. Bobby Jacobs kicked his Scottish terrier when he was in a
bad mood. Mrs. Lester fed fresh salmon to her Siamese cat
Lucky seven days a week. Cats love to gossip, and Sally was
no exception. By August, Keri knew the family secrets of every
cat-owning household in town.

Mew was now able to go up and down the stairs by him-
self, and Sally was more than ready to go outside and have
some fun. "He'll be fine," Sally insisted.

"But he's your baby. How can you leave him?" Keri, like
her brother Dan, had been adopted from Korea. She loved her
parents dearly, but Keri still wondered about her birth mother. "What if Mew gets scared or lonely? He won't know where
you are." After much debate, Sally finally convinced Keri that
it was all right to leave Mew alone for a couple of hours while

they played in the woods. It was a drizzly August day, but Keri didn't mind. On rainy days, the forest glistened. Sally was not particularly fond of getting wet, but she was so excited to be out of the house, she hardly noticed. In fact, she ran so fast that Keri had a hard time keeping up with her.

As they approached the library, Sally stopped suddenly. "Oh my!" she shrieked. "It's him."

"Who?"

"Him. Mew's father."

Sulking around the library stairs, Keri saw a rather muscular, black cat with white markings on his chin, chest, and paws—just like Mew. "He's a hunk!" she exclaimed.

"I know."

Keri watched as Sally sauntered over to her mate and rubbed noses. It was a side of Sally she hadn't seen before. After ten minutes, Keri grew impatient. "Are you guys almost through?" she blurted out.

"I beg your pardon," said the dapper black cat, "but Sally and I have a great deal to discuss. So, if you would be so kind."

"Fine. I'll be in the library," Keri answered, shaking her head. It wasn't until she pulled *The Instincts of Newborn Kittens* off the shelf that it hit her: she had just spoken to another cat. For some reason, she had assumed that Sally was the only cat she could understand. Now her mind raced with possibilities.

That night, Keri shared the news with her family, who were by then very used to hearing about Sally's exploits and not at all surprised by this latest development. Dan, who had been the most skeptical of Keri's abilities, was now her biggest fan.

Once school started in September, he boasted to his seventh-grade friends about his sister's special powers. At first, the boys made fun of him. But Dan would say, "Bring your cat to my house after school and we'll prove it." Keri didn't mind. She loved meeting all the cats Sally had told her about. Each kid came up with questions that only his or her cat could answer. "What's your favorite toy?" "Where did you leave your last hair ball?" The cats enjoyed talking to Keri. She had a way about her that made them feel comfortable. Sometimes their answers were more informative than expected. "Fluffy says her favorite place to sleep is on the refrigerator. There's lots of dust balls there and no one ever cleans."

Word spread throughout the small town about Keri's talent with cats. The first person to employ her officially was Dr. Donna Lundstrom, the town vet. "He ate a blue bow off a baby gift," Keri informed the doctor after interviewing Hal, the Millers' wirehaired tabby.

"I was wondering where that bow went. Bad, Hal. Bad cat," said Mrs. Miller, shaking her index finger.

Once, when the Harrises' cat Muzzy was diagnosed with distemper and Mr. Harris swore to the doctor that *his* cat never went outside, Keri got Muzzy to admit that she sneaked out of the house on numerous occasions. Unfortunately, during her last escape, she had met a crazy raccoon across the street. After Keri's discovery, the Animal Rescue League was called in, and the infected raccoon was caught.

It wasn't until the Thompsons' cat Zorro disappeared that

Keri's professional career—the career she would become famous for—really took off. On a chilly Christmas morning, Scott Thompson pounded his fist against the Tarrs' front door. "He's gone! He disappeared last night. We've looked everywhere!" Scott blurted out, trying to catch his breath.

"Oh dear." Keri's mom began to panic, thinking that Scott meant his baby brother. "Sam's missing?"

"Not Sam. Zorro. Keri, you have to help us. He'll freeze to death."

Immediately, Keri began asking Scott questions: "When did you last see Zorro? Where was he? Were there any other cats in the house who may have seen Zorro leave?" After this initial interrogation, Keri put her dark green fleece vest on over her party dress, grabbed her hat, mittens, and boots, and kissed her parents and two dazed-looking aunts good-bye. "Don't worry, I'll be back before you cut the turkey."

"Hey, wait for me!" Sally called. Keri placed Sally inside the neck of her parka, and they followed the redheaded, freckle-faced boy back to his house at the end of the street. Keri surveyed the Thompsons' living room. The presents under the Christmas tree were still wrapped, and Scott's brother Sam was jumping and pulling at candy canes that dangled from above. Mrs. Thompson, who sat sobbing on the couch in her long brown bathrobe, seemed oblivious. So it was a good thing that Keri arrived when she did, because seconds later, Sam had managed to grab onto one of the striped candies and was about to pull it, and the entire tree, down to the ground. Without hesitating, Keri dove toward the falling mass and caught it before it crushed the now very startled toddler.

Mrs. Thompson cried even louder as she hugged and kissed Keri. "Hey, watch it, lady. You're crushing me," Sally hissed from inside Keri's jacket.

After gently scolding Scott's mom for neglecting to watch her child, Keri got down to business. She learned that Zorro had a mad crush on Juliet, the Gibson's blue-faced Siamese who lived across the street. Keri remembered that her fifth-grade class had held a good-bye party for Cathy Gibson, who was moving to Montana after New Year's Day. "I'll be right back," Keri said.

When Keri arrived, she found the Gibsons' household in utter chaos. Mr. and Mrs. Gibson, Cathy, and her four younger sisters were all sitting on boxes in the kitchen, eating Swanson's turkey TV dinners. Cathy, who had always been very generous, immediately offered Keri half of her apple crisp.

"Thanks, but I'm here on official cat business," Keri replied. "Can I speak with Juliet?" This might have seemed like an odd question. But by now, everyone had heard about Keri's powers.

"Sure, if you can find her," Cathy offered, making a gesture toward the hundreds of boxes that filled their house.

Maybe I should start with Romeo, Keri thought as she eyed Juliet's twin brother happily munching on the scraps of turkey left in one of the aluminum trays. "Romeo, have you seen Juliet?"

"No," Romeo answered without looking up.

"He's lying," Sally whispered.

Keri picked up Romeo and looked him straight in the eyes. "Romeo, where is Juliet?"

"How should I know? She doesn't tell me everything."

He was playing hardball. That was okay—Keri could play hardball, too. She grabbed the TV dinner tray and walked over to the trash. "You want to see these turkey scraps again?" Keri threatened as she stepped on the lever that raised the trash lid.

"Not the turkey!" Romeo cried.

"Then talk."

Romeo admitted that he had seen Juliet squeeze through the cat door the night before. He had asked her where she was going on such a cold night. She had turned to him and in her sultry voice said, "To be with my lover or die," and then disappeared through the flap.

What a diva! Sally thought.

The Gibsons were shocked and a little embarrassed that Juliet had been missing for an entire night without anyone noticing. But with the house in such a state, it was easy to understand. Now they were starting to panic. "Stay calm," Keri instructed everyone. "I'm sure they couldn't have gone too far." Cathy showed Keri the cat door in the garage. Outside, Keri followed Juliet's tracks over a small hill, where they were joined by a second set of paw prints—Zorro's, no doubt. The tracks led into the woods and became increasingly difficult to follow.

"I guess they're gone for good," Sally sighed.

"Sally, we haven't been looking for that long."

"I'm cold and I'm hungry. And I refuse to risk my life for

that little snob."

"Juliet?"

"None of us likes her."

"Well, you can go back to the house if you like, but I'm going to find them!"

Sally grew quiet after that. By now they were approaching the Taylor estate. Mrs. Taylor was a widow. The only time Keri ever saw her was on Halloween. The old woman made brownies for the trick-or-treaters, which Dad promptly threw away because of the "don't-eat-anything-that-isn't-wrapped-and-sealed" rule.

Snow began to fall on Keri's lashes, which blinked trying to follow the tiny paw prints before they completely disappeared in the whiteness. "Sally, I can hardly see the tracks. We can't lose them now."

"What was that?" Sally interrupted, breaking her silence.

"I don't hear anything."

"This way," ordered Sally as she jumped out from the neck of Keri's warm jacket onto the snow and began running around to the other side of the house. Once they turned the corner, Keri could hear cats shrieking. "Hurry, Keri!" Sally called.

The wails were coming from inside a broken-down shed. "Help. Help us, somebody!"

"We'll get you out," Keri panted, out of breath. She inspected every corner of the locked shed, but couldn't find an opening.

"I'm too young to die," cried Juliet.

"Don't worry. I'll go get Mrs. Taylor. She must have the key."

As Keri followed the snow-covered stone path that curved around the far side of the house, visions of the old woman who lived inside raced through her mind. Her crooked nose and small piercing eyes reminded Keri of the witch face on her orange-and-black Halloween bag. "Isn't Mrs. Taylor the one who boils children for breakfast?" asked Sally. Only a month ago, at Keri's birthday sleepover, Jessica had told the group of wide-eyed ten-year-olds the creepy story of the Taylor estate.

"Mrs. Taylor," Jessica had whispered, as she held a flashlight under her chin, "is the reincarnation of a woman who was hanged during the Salem Witch Trials. She came back three hundred years ago to avenge her death, but first she had to sign a pact to eat one child each year. Every Halloween, one unsuspecting girl is mysteriously drawn to her door. She knocks three times and then disappears forever." That night after her party guests had fallen asleep, Keri and Sally vowed never to go trick-or-treating at the Taylor estate again.

"This is Christmas, not Halloween," Keri reassured herself. But as she approached the door, her knees grew weak. She mustered all her strength and finally knocked. It took over five minutes for Mrs. Taylor to make her way down the stairs to the front door, and Sally squirmed inside Keri's vest the entire time. Mrs. Taylor was quite surprised to see a shivering young girl standing on her porch. "You must be freezing. Come inside and warm up. Isn't it lovely of you to visit old Mrs. Taylor on Christmas? What's your name, dear?"

"Keri . . . Keri Tarr."

"Nice to meet you, Keri."

"Nice to meet you, too. I'm sorry to bother you on Christmas, but . . . there are two cats trapped in your shed. And I was wondering if you have the key?"

"Oh my, the key to the shed. I don't know. I must have it somewhere. I haven't opened the shed in over ten years. Bob used to keep his tools in there."

"Is there a place that you keep old keys?"

"Let me see. Why don't you come upstairs to the living room and help me look?"

Sally dug her claws into Keri's shoulder. "Are you crazy? We can't go up there."

"We have to," Keri murmured.

"What was that, dear?"

"Nothing, my cat's hungry. That's all."

"You have a cat with you. I didn't notice. How marvelous. I'll have to introduce him to my Fritzy."

"I'm a *she*. Tell her I'm a *she*."

"My cat's name is Sally," Keri said, walking slowly behind the widow.

"A girl cat. Well, isn't she pretty? Now, come right in here and sit down while I look for that wood box. Fritzy! Come here, sweetheart. Come meet Sally!"

Fritzy was the largest orange-and-white cat that Keri had ever seen. One look at Sally and he hissed so viciously that the small black cat dove back into Keri's vest and started to shake. "Stop that, Fritzy," Mrs. Taylor scolded. "Be nice to our guests. He is always getting into scrapes. Last night some cat tried to rip his ear off. Now, where could that box be? Maybe it's in the kitchen. You just stay here and relax, dear. Fritzy will keep you company. Fritzy, you be nice."

Once Mrs. Taylor left the room, Keri gave Fritzy a piece of her mind. "That was mean scaring Sally like that."

"Yeah, what's it to you," he retorted, pacing back and forth.

"She's my cat. That's what."

"I could rip your arm to shreds with one swipe, girlie."

"The name's Keri. Keri Tarr. And I'm not afraid of you."

Fritzy stopped pacing. "You're . . . Keri Tarr? *The* . . . Keri Tarr?"

"The same."

"Oh, um . . . I apologize, Miss Tarr. I had no idea. I beg your pardon."

"You should say you're sorry to my cat. She's the one you frightened."

"I'm really sorry, Miss . . . um, what's her name?"

"Sally."

"Miss Sally . . . I hope you'll forgive me."

Sally finally poked her head out of Keri's vest and in her haughtiest voice said, "Perhaps. In time."

Keri sighed and looked around the room. There was no tree, no presents, not even a card in sight. *Maybe she's Jewish,* Keri thought. Her Grandma Caryl and Grandpa Herb celebrated Hanukkah instead of Christmas.

"Keri," called Mrs. Taylor from the kitchen. "Could you give me a hand in here, dear?" As Keri entered the kitchen, she observed that there were no pots or pans cooking on the stove, not even a turkey TV dinner in the oven. Mrs. Taylor stood over a large wooden box that must have contained a hundred keys.

"Oh my," Keri exclaimed as she gazed in the box.

"Yes," agreed Mrs. Taylor. "There are so many."

Keri had taken a good look at the lock in the shed door, so she knew that they were looking for an old skeleton key. She and Mrs. Taylor sorted out each skeleton key—twelve in all. "I'll be right back."

As they descended the staircase, Keri told Sally, "This won't be so bad."

"Unless none of them fits the shed."

"Oh, yeah." Keri placed the twelve possible keys in her pocket and headed out the door, followed by Fritzy. Through her kitchen window, Mrs. Taylor could barely see them crossing her backyard through the clouds of blowing snow.

At the shed, Keri tried the keys one at a time. "How did you guys get in here anyway?"

"Juliet and I were making our escape when a loathsome bandit cat attacked us."

Fritzy drooped his head. "I guess that would be me."

"My Zorro fought so bravely."

"I cut that cat's ear with my claw."

"He was wonderful. But I got scared. I saw a hole at the base of the shed and crawled right through it."

"I dashed in after her."

"But a big piece of wood fell from the wall."

"The entrance was blocked."

27

Just then, one of the dozen keys that Keri tried slid into the lock. "I've got it!" she said. But the key wouldn't turn. "Oh no, it's frozen. I need a lighter."

"I'll get one," Fritzy volunteered. Keri and Sally just stared at him. "It's the least I can do." And he ran back to the house.

"So why did you two run away in the first place?" asked Sally.

"They were going to take my beloved Juliet away from me."

"I didn't want to live without Zorro."

"Wow, now that's true love," Sally sighed.

Fritzy bounded back over the snow with the lighter in his mouth. Keri quickly melted the ice inside the lock and opened the door.

"Oh . . . that's the fiend who attacked us," cried Juliet glaring at the huge tiger-striped cat before her.

Keri gave Fritzy a nudge with her boot. "Go on."

"I'm really sorry I pounced on you guys."

"And . . . ," prodded Keri.

"And . . . I promise not to do it again."

Keri and the four cats made their way back to Mrs. Taylor's living room, but no one said a word to Fritzy along the way. Keri phoned the Thompsons, the Gibsons and her own parents from Mrs. Taylor's kitchen. As she and Mrs. Taylor waited for the cars to arrive, Keri finally got up the courage to ask, "So are you going anywhere for Christmas?"

"Me, oh no. I'll just stay here."

"Are you Jewish?"

"No dear, I'm Episcopalian."

"Well, is your family coming over?"

"Heavens no. They all live too far away."

"Oh." And they sat in silence for about three minutes.

Suddenly the doorbell rang and the house was full of people. "Juliet!" cried Cathy.

"Zorro, you bad pussycat, come here," whined Mrs. Thompson, who was still wearing her bathrobe.

They all thanked Keri over and over again and then said their good-byes. Cathy Gibson was halfway out the door when Juliet leaped from her arms and dashed straight under

Mrs. Taylor's couch. Before Mrs. Thompson could grab him, Zorro followed suit.

"Juliet. Juliet, come out from there." Cathy pleaded.

"Not again!" cried Mrs. Thompson. "Zorro, come on, sweetie. It's time to come home." The cats wouldn't budge.

Just then, Keri realized what had to be done. She asked everyone to sit down. After forty-five minutes of intense negotiation and a torrent of tears, Cathy Gibson finally agreed to let the Thompsons adopt Juliet.

"We still have Romeo," Mrs. Gibson said gently as she wiped a tear from Cathy's face.

"I know," Cathy muttered.

"And you can visit her next year when we come back for Grandma's birthday."

Cathy gave Juliet a long hug good-bye, and the Gibsons returned to their stacks of cardboard boxes.

"Let's go home," Keri finally said. But she stopped before they reached the door. "Mom, could I ask Mrs. Taylor and Fritzy to come over for Christmas dinner?"

"Sure."

The turkey was a little cold, but no one cared. Mrs. Taylor told the Tarrs all about when she had served as an army nurse in Europe during World War II, which was how she met Mr. Taylor. After dinner, Keri and Dan played their rendition of "Boogie Woogie Bugle Boy" (Keri on saxophone, and Dan on piano). Everyone sang along, but Mrs. Taylor was the only one who really knew all the words. Aunt Wendy and Auntie Diane started dancing, and soon the entire family was up on their feet, including Sally. Mew watched, his tail twitching in time with the music.

"Um, Miss Sally, may I have the next dance?" Fritzy pleaded.

"Not if you were the last cat in the neighborhood," she replied, and she continued to dance by herself. Sally danced her way up the stairs, through the attic, and out onto the rooftop. Fritzy followed her and for a moment Sally became so caught up in the rhythm that she let him swing her to and fro. But as soon as the music ended, Sally regained her composure. "This never happened," she said, and then she disappeared into the basement. For the rest of the evening Fritzy trailed behind Sally, begging for forgiveness. But all she would say was: "Perhaps. In time."

That night, after Keri and Sally were asleep, Dan went down to his father's shop in the basement. He used his father's tools to fashion an oblong piece of wood and carefully carve a design around the border. He spent hours painting intricate letters in gold leaf. When his sister woke up the next morning, she was surprised to see a blue-and-gold sign hanging outside her bedroom door. The sign read: KERI TARR: CAT DETECTIVE.

4

The case of the Soderberg cats

Keri had never heard of Mrs. Soderberg before, and neither had Sally. But the eccentric old woman had lived less than three miles away. When she died, no one came to her funeral. She had no friends, no relatives, and no one to remember the hundred and ten cats who lived inside the Soderberg house. Mrs. Soderberg passed away quietly in her hospital bed. When her neighbors realized she was gone, they immediately called town officials and demanded that the dilapidated Soderberg house be condemned.

Twenty-two-year-old Mallory Connors led the campaign to knock the old building down. The tall, neatly dressed blonde had grown up next door to the crumbling mass and couldn't bear the thought of looking at it one day longer than she had to. And so the windows were boarded up, NO TRESPASSING signs were posted, and the house was scheduled to be demolished. The hundred and ten cats inside had no idea of this looming danger. They had other concerns. No one had fed them in over two weeks, and they wondered why Mrs.

Soderberg had deserted them. In truth, they would have died of starvation, if not for an unexpected turn of events.

It was a Wednesday afternoon in April, and Keri was at soccer practice. Sally loved to watch Keri play and used to chase the ball—that is, until Kimmy Sandler accidentally kicked her in the middle of a game. Since then, Sally was content to sit and watch. On this particular day, Kimmy kicked a foul ball straight into the woods and out of sight. "I'll get it," said Keri. "Come on, Sally. You can help me."

The ground was still cold, though most of the snow had melted. Keri could smell the swamp nearby, which had started to thaw. *I hope it didn't fall into the muck,* she thought.

Sally didn't like the sensation of cold mud beneath her paws. "It's gone," she announced.

"It couldn't have just disappeared. Keep looking."

"I'm looking. I'm looking." Sally shook each paw and continued down the path.

Keri's running shoes were starting to sink in the mud. As she turned to head the other way, she saw something round, like a soccer ball. "Sally, I think it's over there, behind that tree."

Sally arrived at the tree before Keri could traipse through the mud. "Uh . . . Keri."

"Did you find it?"

"I found something." Sally was staring straight into the eyes of a Maine Coon cat five times her size.

The massive hulk of mud-caked gray fur was trembling. Keri arrived at the scene just in time to hear him utter, in a thick southern drawl, "I'd be much obliged, Miss . . ." He paused to catch his breath. "If you could save the others."

"What others?"

But before he could say another word, the polite cat passed out. Keri wasted no time in picking him up and running to Dr. Lundstrom's office a few blocks away. She watched as the vet examined the ailing cat and inserted an intravenous line into his front leg. "This cat is dehydrated. I don't think he's been fed in a while," Dr. Lundstrom said, shaking her head. "This should help." She then placed the cat in a small room with extra oxygen.

It was hard for Keri to fight back tears. "Can I stay here for a while?" she pleaded. Dr. Lundstrom called Keri's mom, who drove right over.

After two hours, Mom said, "Sweetheart, it's dinnertime. We should go home."

"No, Mom, I can't leave. I have to save the others."

"What others?"

"That's the problem. I don't know."

Mom finally agreed to let Keri stay there overnight with Dr. Lundstrom. And although Keri wasn't very hungry, she ate half of a peanut butter sandwich, to make her mother happy. Sally, on the other hand, was thrilled that she had a wide selection of cat food from which to choose. "I think I'll have tuna and cheese . . . no, no make that seafood supreme." That night, Keri and Sally sat by the plastic door to the special oxygen cage. They fell asleep listening to the drip of saline as it made its way down the tube and into the large gray cat.

Early the next morning, Sally heard a faint mewing. "Wake up, Keri!" Keri opened her eyes.

The gray cat was still weak, but had managed to sit up. "Were you able to save the others?" he asked.

Keri woke up Dr. Lundstrom, who was sleeping on the couch in her waiting room. After examining her patient, she allowed Keri to question him. Keri discovered that the cat's name was Beau, and that he was originally from New Orleans. More importantly, Beau told her about the Soderberg house—how the other cats were still trapped inside with no one to feed them, and how he had escaped. It was yesterday afternoon and the cats were huddled together, weak from hunger, when a boy broke into the house. He had pried the door open and stepped inside. When the cats saw him, they thought they'd been saved. They meowed and meowed, begging for food, but the boy just smirked, turned around, and left. Beau mustered all his strength and bolted to the door. The boy kicked him, trying to shut him inside, but Beau pushed his way past the boy's boot and ran into the woods. There he wandered until his strength ran out. He lay down by a tree and stayed there until Sally found him.

Had it been another boy, any boy other than Kurt Cooper, the cats would have been saved. Any other boy would have told his parents or contacted the police, but not Kurt. No, Kurt ran home with a different plan. He waited until his parents went to bed, and then he snuck into his older brother's room. There, very quietly, he opened his brother's closet door, reached up high, and removed a shoebox from the top shelf.

He tiptoed back to his room and opened the box. Inside was a BB gun. The same gun his brother used to kill a bird. The gun his mother thought had been thrown out. Kurt grinned as he placed the gun and bag of pellets into his backpack, and then he went to sleep.

As Keri questioned Beau on the whereabouts of the Soderberg house, Mallory Connors drove to Town Hall. She was on a mission and nothing could stop her. "I have been waiting over a week," she sniped at Miss Gardiner, the befuddled town clerk. "The house is still there!"

"These things take time."

"Time? My wedding is this Saturday. I will not have my guests starring at that run-down, flea-infested rattrap. Is that clear?" Poor Miss Gardiner tried to reason with the bride-to-be. She calmly explained that the demolition was scheduled for next month. But Mallory Connors would not give up. She ranted and raved until Miss Gardiner picked up the phone, dialed the number of a local construction company, and made arrangements. The town would have to pay extra for the rush order, but the offending eyesore would be knocked down by noon. Without so much as a thank-you, Mallory Connors turned around and huffed and puffed her way out of the office.

There were two students missing from Miss Clifford's class that day, Keri Tarr and Kurt Cooper. Keri's mom had called the school, so Miss Clifford knew that the Cat Detective was solving an important case. But where was Kurt? She shook her head. It was Kurt's fifth absence that month. Kurt had walked to the bus stop that morning, but as soon as his mother drove past him on her way to work, Kurt took off. He followed a path through the woods to the Soderberg house—the BB gun tucked away in his backpack. He began to fantasize about shooting all the cats. It would be like a video game. And later, when he was through, he would show off his dirty work. All the kids at school feared him, and he liked it that way. This latest escapade would serve as a warning to anyone who even thought about challenging him. If he could shoot a bunch of cats, what else might he be capable of?

When Keri told Dr. Lundstrom that over a hundred cats were trapped in an abandoned house, she immediately called the Animal Rescue League. They agreed to send a team of veterinarians with enough pet taxis to handle an unspecified number of casualties. Then Dr. Lundstrom drove Keri and Sally to the Soderberg house. Keri held Sally tight as she tried to prepare herself for what she was about to see. *What if we're too late? What if they're all dead?* Keri couldn't bear the thought of it.

Mallory Connors was the first to arrive at the Soderberg house. There she waited impatiently for a bulldozer to arrive. *If it's not here by noon,* she thought, *I'll call and give that Miss Gardiner a piece of my mind. Where are they?* She looked in one direction, and then the other, which is why she didn't notice Kurt crossing the front lawn and slipping into the house. Unable to wait until noon, she flipped open her cell phone and called information. "Town Hall. Bolton." She waited for the number.

Inside, the cats could barely move. They mewed softly,

looking up at Kurt with their innocent eyes. He felt a twinge of guilt over what he was about to do, but then shook it off. *This will shut them up,* he thought as he unzipped his backpack. He opened the bag of pellets and started to load the gun.

"What took you so long?" Miss Connors yelled at the mustachioed man driving a large yellow bulldozer into the driveway. She folded her phone and tossed it inside her purse. The man turned off the engine and started surveying the house. "What are you waiting for," Miss Connors shouted as she followed him around the house. "Just knock the thing down!" Her high heels were now stuck in the mud.

"Look lady, you don't just knock something down without checking it out. What are you, the owner or something?"

"*Me?* The owner of *this?*" She was disgusted by the man's stupidity. "I own that blue colonial next door." She yanked one shoe out of the dirt and then the other.

"Well, unless you like getting covered in sludge, you better go back to your own house." The man climbed back into the bulldozer and started to roll toward the house.

Mallory Connors was not used to being spoken to in such a rude manner. She was about to threaten the man with some horrible thing or other when Dr. Lundstrom's station wagon barreled down the driveway nearly hitting the bulldozer. "Hey! Watch it, lady," the man shouted as he hit the brakes.

Keri jumped out of the backseat and ran to the house, followed by Sally. She thought she'd have to bust down the door, so she was surprised that it was unlocked. She was even more surprised to find Kurt Cooper inside, aiming a BB gun at a helpless bunch of cats. "Stop!" she screamed.

Kurt was startled by her voice, but he quickly recovered. "Get out of here."

"Not until you give me that gun."

"Maybe I should shoot you," he snarled.

"The cats haven't done anything to you, Kurt."

"Oh, I forgot. You're the big 'Cat Detective.' What are you going to do, arrest me?"

Kurt aimed his gun at one of the cats and was about to shoot when Keri lunged at him. Caught off balance, Kurt accidentally pulled the trigger releasing a pellet toward the ceiling. As he tumbled to the floor, Keri dove towards the gun in his hand, but Kurt rolled out of reach. All of a sudden, the ceiling started to shake. The pellet had hit an already loose hook that supported a dusty chandelier above. Keri had just enough time to push Kurt out of the way and grab Sally before the antique chandelier came crashing down. As glass exploded in the air, Keri held Sally safely beneath her. The Soderberg cats scurried to every corner of the house—under beds, sofas, chairs, anywhere they could find. One cat leaped on a velvet chair, causing it to topple over Keri. Mrs. Soderberg's quaint living room had turned into a war zone. Keri buried her face in Sally's fur, and waited for the particles of glass to settle.

When it was over, Kurt sat up—stunned.

"Are you okay?" Keri asked, peeking out from under the stuffed chair.

Kurt stood slowly and surveyed the damage. For a moment, he considered moving the heavy chair off Keri, but then a darker, more sinister thought entered his mind. He clutched the gun tightly in his hand. "Thanks for the help, Keri. It was too easy before. Now I get to hunt for them. That's much more fun." Kurt began to stalk the cats, crushing pieces of crystal beneath his boots. He spied a frail tabby under the loveseat. "Come here, kitty, kitty," he whispered coyly.

As Kurt aimed his BB gun, Keri struggled to get out from under the chair, but it wouldn't budge. "Don't do this!" she pleaded.

"That's it," Kurt said, perfecting his aim. "I've got you now."

Suddenly, the large man from the bulldozer stepped inside. "I wouldn't do that if I were you," he said as he grabbed Kurt's arm. Kurt tried to run, but he slipped on the broken glass, cutting his palms.

Just then a dozen or more vets from the Animal Rescue League piled into the house. It took nearly an hour to locate all the cats that had hid during the explosion. Keri had to assure each of them that the uniformed men and women were there to help. While Dr. Lundstrom wrapped Kurt's hands in bandages to stop the bleeding, Keri tried to comfort the cats.

"Where's our mom? Where's Mrs. Soderberg?" two tiny black cats mewed to Keri as she held them on her lap.

Keri didn't want break the sad news to them when they were in such a sickly state. "I'll find out and tell you later," she said gently. Keri learned that the twin sisters were named Gerta and Eloise. She made sure to memorize their faces for later.

"I'm so hungry!" moaned a multi-colored cat named Fred.

"Don't worry," Keri said scratching behind his left ear. "Soon, you'll have all the food you can eat."

Finally, the vets had loaded all the cats into pet taxis and were on their way to the animal hospital. "Dr. Lundstrom, do you think they'll be all right?" Keri asked.

"I hope so, Keri."

Suddenly, Sally popped up from under the couch. "Where'd everybody go?

The man with the bulldozer—who liked to be called Big Bill—offered to drive Kurt to the hospital, where he had a good long talk with Kurt's parents. Mallory Connors stood screaming in the driveway as the bulldozer rode away, but no one paid any attention. Inside, Keri and Sally investigated the old house. Black-and-white photographs of Mrs. Soderberg and her cats lined the walls. There were beautifully painted cat murals on the ceilings. Keri ventured upstairs and into Mrs. Soderberg's bedroom. A canopy bed took up one side of the room, and there was an antique dresser by the window. In the opposite corner of the room was an elaborate dressing table and mirror. Keri noticed a large yellow envelope on the table with the words, TO WHOM IT MAY CONCERN, written upon it. She brought the envelope downstairs. "Should I open it?" she asked the vet.

"Sure. You found it."

Keri tore the envelope, and pulled out a bankbook and an unusually long piece of paper on which was written:

*If you have found this will and testament, I am
most likely dead. I hereby leave my house and the sum*

of two million dollars to the Humane Society, on the following conditions: 1. That my house is renovated and turned into an animal shelter. 2. That each of my cats is placed in a good and loving home.

This is my dying wish. Amelia Soderberg.

That afternoon, Keri and Sally visited the animal hospital with Dr. Lundstrom. They brought Beau with them. After a checkup, he was reunited with the rest of the Soderberg cats, who were all on the road to recovery.

"Come on, Keri," said Dr. Lundstrom closing her medical bag. "I'll drive you home."

As they drove past the hospital exit sign, Keri opened the yellow envelope and reread its contents. "What should we do with this?" she asked the vet.

"I'm not sure, Keri. I think we need a lawyer."

The next day, Keri, Sally, and Dr. Lundstrom met with a young attorney named Ms. Nevans to review Mrs. Soderberg's will. After reading it carefully, Ms. Nevans took off her wire-rimmed glasses and shook her head. "I've got to warn you, converting an old estate like the Soderbergs' into an animal shelter . . . well it's going to be a major headache. Are you sure you want to do this?"

"Of course we're sure," Keri blurted out.

Dr. Lundstrom took a deep breath and exhaled. "We're sure. Do you think you can help us?"

"Me? I don't usually deal with real estate. And I'm very busy just now. You'd be much better off with another attorney. I can make some calls."

Just then Sally jumped on Ms. Nevans's desk. "I'll handle this," she said, with a wink to Keri. Sally rubbed her cheek on a box of pens and started to purr.

"What an adorable cat!" Ms. Nevans exclaimed as she petted Sally's nose. "Oh, Keri, can I hold her?"

"Go ahead."

From that point on, Ms. Nevans took care of all their legal matters. And she was right about the challenges they would face. Plans had to be drafted, permits secured, and bids from contractors reviewed. Dr. Lundstrom postponed a well-deserved vacation to oversee the project, and Keri helped her every step of the way. She kept track of documents, made phone calls, and when it came time for the citizens of Bolton to vote on the proposal, Keri gave an impassioned speech about animal rights.

Finally construction started and everyone was happy. Well, almost everyone. Mallory Connors tried to sue the town for refusing to tear down the old house, causing her untold emotional hardship. But the case was thrown out of court, and she and her new husband moved to California.

As for Kurt, he began seeing the school counselor Ms. Pedersen on a regular basis. She, along with his parents and the man with the bulldozer, devised a plan for Kurt. Despite his earsplitting protests, every weekend Kurt had to help clear downed trees and overgrown shrubs. After a month or so, Kurt started to look forward to Saturdays with Big Bill— though he would never admit it.

And the Soderberg cats? Once Beau was cleaned up and groomed, Dr. Lundstrom thought he was the handsomest, most dashing cat she'd ever seen, so she adopted him. And after a few days in the hospital, the hundred and nine *other* cats were feeling much better. Keri visited them every day. When it was time, she made sure that Mrs. Soderberg's dying wish was fulfilled. It took several weeks. Keri interviewed each cat to discover its likes and dislikes, personality and so forth. She placed ads in the local paper, and then spoke to each applicant *in their home*—just to be sure. She made long lists of cats and people, and after comparing them, matched them up. Gerta and Eloise were adopted by Miss Gardiner, the town clerk. While they missed Mrs. Soderberg, they were content with their new owner. Fred went to live with Ms. Nevans and her three corgis, two hamsters and one very talkative cockatiel. After all the Soderberg cats were placed, Keri visited them one more time. Finally, she was satisfied—each and every cat had a good and loving home.

5

Madeleine disappears

By June, Keri had solved over a dozen cases of missing cats. She knew each of the town's firefighters by name and had even received a plaque for "Outstanding Service to the Community" from the Town Council. Dan acted as her business agent, as she now charged a fee of five dollars a day, plus expenses. Keri donated all her proceeds to the Soderberg Animal Shelter, which had named the section of building that housed cats the Keri Tarr Wing.

Although business was booming, Keri grew impatient. "Where's the challenge?" she complained to Sally one day as she rode her bike home from her saxophone lesson. Keri had become so good at her job that she could solve a case with barely a thought.

"You're not thinking of quitting?" Sally asked, bouncing in the front basket of Keri's bike. Sally loved the limelight. She was, after all, the most famous cat in town.

"No, of course not," Keri assured her, "but I wish I could get just one case that was . . . I don't know . . . really hard." Keri stopped riding long enough to readjust the saxophone case that was strapped to her back. She pulled her blue skirt with tiny silver and maroon flowers up over her seat so that it wouldn't get caught in the spokes, and then continued home.

When she walked into the house, Mew wound around her legs. He had grown into a fine young cat who loved to swat at moths and other flying insects in the back yard. Keri wanted a snack, and in the kitchen, she found a note on the counter: "Keri, I took Dan to the dentist. There are some fresh strawberries in the fridge. Be back around 5:00. Love, Mom." *Strawberries,* Keri thought, *yum.* But before she could unbuckle the strap to her music case, the phone rang. "I'll get it," Keri yelled, forgetting that she was the only one home.

"Hello."

"Keri, is . . . that . . . you?" The voice on the other end shook.

"It's me. Is this Aunt Wendy?"

"Oh, thank goodness you're there. You have to help me."

"What's wrong?"

"It's Madeleine. She's gone. She's never run away before, not even for a night. Something must have happened to her. What am I going to do?"

Keri gave her standard reply in these situations: "Don't worry. I'll be right there." And she hung up. It wasn't until she put Sally in the basket of her bike and started riding down the street that she remembered that Aunt Wendy lived in Boston.

"Boston!" Sally exclaimed. "You can't ride your bike to Boston."

Sally was right. It was too far. And even though she had been to Aunt Wendy's apartment before, she didn't have a clue how to get there. "We need a map," she decided, and pulled into the library parking lot. "Miss Owen . . ."

"Yes, Keri?"

"If you had to go to Boston, and you didn't have a car, how would you get there?"

"Oh, I suppose I'd take the commuter line and then transfer to the T at Back Bay. Where in Boston do you need to go?"

"Jamaica Plain."

"Jamaica Plain . . . let's see." She pulled out a subway map and found three stops on the Orange Line located in that neighborhood. "Is there a particular street?"

Keri thought for a moment. "Rockview Street."

"Rockview . . ." Miss Owen opened a large map of Boston and checked the index. "C-3," she said, and then searched the corresponding square on the map. "Oh, here it is, Rockview Street. You need to get off here at Stony Brook Station. Then walk down this street, turn left on Chestnut, right on Spring Park, and left again on Rockview."

"Thank you, Miss Owen. Could I please borrow those maps?"

"Of course, Keri, but can't your mother drive you there?"

"She's at the dentist with Dan. I can't wait. It's a cat emergency."

"I see. Does your mother know you're going to Boston by yourself?"

"Sally's coming with me. We're going to my Aunt Wendy's apartment."

"Oh, your aunt. Well, I suppose that's all right."

"Thanks for the maps, Miss Owen. I'll bring them back tomorrow."

"No rush, dear. Be careful."

When Keri got back on her bike, she thought about what Miss Owen had said. "We better leave Mom a note."

"Keri, how much does it cost to take the train?" Sally asked, hoping it would be more than she had.

"I forgot to ask." Back at the house, Keri ran to the cigar box where she kept all her earnings before giving them to the shelter. "Thirty-five dollars. That should be enough," she said, stuffing the bills into the pocket of her green vest. Then she took a marker from the kitchen drawer and wrote: "One of Aunt Wendy's cats is missing. Have taken the train to Boston. *Don't worry*. I'll be back soon. Love, Keri," and taped it to the breezeway door. But as soon as Keri and Sally turned the corner of their street, a huge gust of wind blew the piece of paper off the door and far away from sight.

Keri, who still had her saxophone strapped to her back, rode as fast as she could to the commuter rail station. "Can I take my bike on the train?" she asked the man behind the glass window.

"Yeah, yeah, go on," he said, puffing on his pipe.

The train came almost immediately, and Keri struggled to get her bike, Sally, and the saxophone all aboard safely. "Now this is an adventure," she told Sally, who was not entirely convinced that she liked riding on a train.

Once they reached Back Bay, Keri found the entrance to the Orange Line, and after asking a young woman with purple hair and a black, leather-studded jacket which side of the platform to stand on, Keri managed to get on the right train.

"Stony Brook," the conductor soon announced.

"That's us," Keri said with a big smile on her face. "Now, let's look at that map. Down this street, left on Chestnut, right on Spring Park. Rockview Street. Here it is."

"Do we know what house on Rockview Street?" Sally asked.

"Yes," Keri answered, pushing her bike up the steep hill. "I helped Aunt Wendy move in. It's . . . that one." She was pointing at a white, three-story house with a magnolia tree in the front yard. Keri pushed the top buzzer next to her aunt's name.

Aunt Wendy rushed downstairs to let them in. "Oh, Keri, thank you for coming, I just don't know what I would have done." Keri locked her bike to the railing of the front porch. "You didn't ride your bike all the way from Bolton, did you?"

"Oh no," Keri replied. "We took the T."

"Have you done that before?" Aunt Wendy asked as she led Keri up to her rooftop apartment.

"No, but it was easy to figure out."

"Not for me. Can I get you some water or juice?"

"Juice, please."

"Hello? Water? I'm thirsty, too," Sally added.

"Aunt Wendy, can Sally have some water?"

"Oh, of course. Here you go, Sally. Oh, she looks just like my Madeleine."

Actually, Madeleine weighed twice as much as Sally, but Keri decided not to correct her aunt. "Let's get down to business. You still have Jessie, right?"

"Yes, he's been hiding under the bed ever since Madeleine disappeared."

"I see. And exactly when was that?"

"Yesterday afternoon. I called the cats in when it started to rain, but only Jessie came. Madeleine hates being out in the rain." Aunt Wendy started to cry.

"Now, you have to stay calm. You say Jessie's under the bed."

"He hasn't even come out to eat."

"He must know something. You mind if Sally and I have a word with him?"

Aunt Wendy showed Keri and Sally into the bedroom. "It might be better if we spoke to him in private," Keri said. And her aunt left them alone in the room.

Jessie, who had long brownish black fur with patches of white on his chest and paws, was shaking. Keri and Sally tried everything they could think of to get him to talk, but the only thing he would say was, "It's all my f . . . f . . . fault."

Finally, Sally crawled under the bed and started licking his ear. "You're such a brave, handsome cat," she cooed. "I know you would do anything to help save Madeleine. So why don't you tell me and Keri what you know?" Keri was shocked. She had never seen Sally act this nice to any cat (besides the hunk). It worked. Jessie crawled out from under the bed.

Once he started, Jessie told them every detail of what had happened the day before. The two of them were outside. Madeleine was basking in the sun as usual, while he roamed through the neighbors' lawns. Jessie had a group of cat friends he liked to hang out with. Madeleine refused to associate with any of them, and she rarely left the deck. Yesterday, as Jessie approached his pals, he heard them gossiping about Artaud Félon, the meanest, toughest cat in Paris—maybe the world. Word spread that Félon had been challenged to a duel by none other than Madeleine's brother Jules.

Jules moved to Paris with Aunt Wendy's friend Michèle after she quit her job as a French teacher at the Waring School, north of Boston. Madeleine still idolized him, and went on and on about her handsome, brave, suave, intelligent brother in Paris. And she always managed to throw in some remark about how Jessie could never be half the cat her brother was. Because of this, Jessie hated Jules. He couldn't wait to tell Madeleine that her beloved Jules was about to fight a cat so vicious that he had a reputation for killing anyone who dared to cross him. "I w . . . w . . . wanted to make her cry for m . . . m . . . making me feel bad. But w . . . w . . . when I told her, she said, 'Poor Jules. I have to save him,' and r . . . r . . . ran out into the street."

"Where did she go?" Keri asked.

"I d . . . d . . . don't know," Jessie whined. "To s . . . s . . . save her brother."

"But how would she get to Paris?"

"I t . . . told you, I don't know. Oh, it's all my f . . . f . . . fault."

Keri got the names of Jessie's friends and where they hung out. "Aunt Wendy, does Madeleine have a brother named Jules?"

"Well, yes. He lives in Paris with my friend Michèle. How did you know that?"

"Do you have Michèle's phone number?"

"In Paris? I suppose I do. But what does this have to do with Madeleine?"

"I don't have time to explain. Can you call her?"

"Now? It's past midnight there."

"I need to speak to her right away."

"If you say so." Aunt Wendy looked up Michèle's number in her address book and dialed. "Hello, Michèle . . . This is Wendy from Boston. Did I wake you up? . . . Sorry. It's about Jules . . . He did? So did Madeleine . . . Look, my niece needs to talk to you. She's a cat detective. Hold on."

Keri learned that Jules had been missing for a week without a trace. She wrote down Michèle's address and phone number just in case, then hung up the phone. "Okay, I need to get some information from some of Jessie's friends in the neighborhood. You wait here. I'll let you know when I find out anything."

"But—"

"Oh, and could you call my mom and tell her I'll be home later than I thought?"

"Of course, but I—"

"I'll explain everything when I get back." And she picked up Sally and was gone.

When Keri's mom received the call from Aunt Wendy, she was mad. But more than that, she was worried. She had never seen the note Keri left her. And how could her sister have let

Keri leave the house alone. In Boston! "She said she'd be back soon," Aunt Wendy offered, trying to calm her sister down. Within an hour, Dan and Keri's mom and dad were at Aunt Wendy's door. After searching the neighborhood, Keri's mom called the police, who put out an all-points bulletin on Keri and Sally. "She seemed like she knew what she was doing," Aunt Wendy said weakly.

"She's ten years old!" shouted Keri's dad.

"There's no point yelling at each other," Dan interrupted. "All we can do is wait."

Meanwhile, Keri had already interviewed Jessie's pals. Snuffles told her that Madeleine was last seen on Chestnut Street. Ginger advised her to find Leonardo, the oldest cat in the neighborhood. Everyone knew and respected Leonardo, even Madeleine.

Keri found Leonardo rummaging through trash cans behind a purple house on Chestnut Street. He was a large black-and-white cat with a scar on his nose and a missing fang on the left side of his mouth. "Yeah, Madeleine came to see me yesterday about her brother Jules. She wanted to know how to get to Paris."

"Did you tell her?" Keri asked.

"Sure, why not? She's a nice kid. The cats around here just don't understand her."

"What did you tell her?"

"You want to go to Paris, you got to get to Logan Airport."

"But how would she get to the airport?"

"Easy. I get the word out to my friend Max. He hangs with

a taxi driver named Joe who does trips back and forth to the airport. They live right over there, in that ugly yellow house. So last night, when Joe opens the car door to let Max in, Madeleine jumps in, too. Joe don't mind that kind of thing. One cat more or less."

"But what happened when Madeleine got to the airport?"

"Hey, that's Max's territory. You better ask him."

"Thanks, Leonardo. You've been a great help. Hasn't he, Sally?" But Sally was too dazed by Leonardo to say a word.

"What a cat," Sally sighed as they reached the front gate.

Keri was about to get on her bike when she saw a black-and-white taxi pull into the driveway across the street. "Is your name

Joe?" she asked the gray-haired cabbie behind the wheel.

"It is."

"And is that Max?" she said, pointing to mangy gray cat beside him.

"Yeah, why?" Keri told him the whole story as quickly as she could. Luckily for her, Joe and Max had a good rapport, and he had no trouble believing her. In fact, Keri learned that certain cabbies like Joe, who were particularly intuitive, understood cats. "Why cabbies?" she asked.

"Why not?" Joe answered with a shrug. "So Keri, what can I do for you?"

"Could you please drive me and Sally to the airport? I can pay you."

"You don't need to give me money. I'll take you there. But I don't think that bike's going to fit."

"Can I bring my saxophone?"

"Oh, sure. No problem."

Keri locked up her bike in Joe's driveway, and then she and Sally jumped into the cab. On the way to Logan Airport, she questioned the gray cat. Max, it turned out, was an old "baggage cat." When he was young, he used to fly all over the world by hiding in the luggage compartments of airplanes. He wasn't the only one. Every day, thousands of cats stow away on flights to and from every possible destination you could think of. After a few years, Max started getting airsick. He figured that he'd seen it all, done it all, and now he just wanted to settle down and be looked after. So one day, when he was hanging out by the taxi stand at Logan, he decided to jump in the next cab that came along. It was Joe's cab, and they'd been together ever since.

"Madeleine, now, she is one determined cat. I'll tell you that. She is going to rescue her brother or die trying," Max told them. "I got her on a direct flight to Paris. She should be there by now."

"I've got to get her back," Keri insisted. "She's my Aunt Wendy's cat. She's worried sick."

"Well, I never arranged for no kid to stow away. I don't know."

"I have thirty-two dollars left. Maybe I can buy a ticket."

"That ain't going to get you to Paris, Keri. Besides, you need a passport, and special papers for your cat. They'd put her in quarantine as soon as the plane landed."

"What's quarantine?" Sally asked.

"That's when they lock you up for months," Max said. "They did it to me once. Never again."

"I'm not going there!" Sally cried, crawling under the car seat.

"Don't worry," said Max. "I'll figure out some way to smuggle you on board."

The taxi pulled up to the curb at Logan Airport, and Keri and Max jumped out. It took some coaxing to convince Sally to come out from under the seat, but when Keri threatened to leave without her, she changed her mind. Keri thanked Joe as she strapped her saxophone case to her back. "This way," Max called. And Keri and Sally followed him into the airport parking lot, and then through a series of narrow tunnels under

Terminal E. The cats ran quickly, but it was a tight squeeze for Keri. She had to hold her breath as she passed around each corner.

At last they came to the runway. They hid behind a large truck filled with luggage. Keri watched as men in overalls loaded the bags onto a plane that had AIR FRANCE written across it. "Now we wait till they're done throwing them in."

"Are you sure this is safe?" asked Keri, who was starting to get scared for the first time.

"Safe as catnip. We just have to wait till they turn their backs . . . Ready . . . Hold on . . . Not quite yet . . . Almost . . . Now! Run!"

Keri picked Sally up and ran as fast as she could to the opening of the baggage hold. She jumped inside before anyone saw her and braced herself as the huge metal door clanged shut behind her. She felt the vibration of the engine as it started to roar. "What about Mew?" Sally cried. "I didn't even say good-bye."

"Hold on, Sally." The plane started down the runway, and before they knew it, they were in the air and on their way to Paris. "I think I need a nap." And with that, Keri and Sally lay down on the softest bag they could find, and fell fast asleep.

6

The baggage cats

When Keri woke up, she found herself surrounded not only by hundreds of suitcases and bags, but also by a motley crew of twenty-seven cats. "Sally," she whispered, "wake up." There were cats of every color and size. But they had two things in common: all of them were scruffy, and they were all staring at Keri. It made her feel a little . . . uncomfortable. "Hi," she finally said, "I'm Keri Tarr."

"*Mais, oui.* We know who you are," hissed a white-and-chocolate Siamese named Charlotte.

"You do?"

"You are *famosa,*" added Puccini, a tortoiseshell tabby with a white patch on his nose.

"*Da,* we know you are following Madeleine to Paris," said Ivan, cocking his bluish gray head.

By now Sally was awake enough to realize that she and Keri weren't alone. She tried to bolt out of Keri's arms, but Keri held on tight. "It's all right, Sally. They're not going to hurt us." Sally didn't believe that for a second.

"You know Madeleine?" Keri asked her captivated audience.

"*Nyet,*" said the Russian blue. "I was not on that flight. But

I know about her."

"Has anyone seen her in Paris?"

"Oui," answered Charlotte. "Houdini saw her at *Les Jardins*, oh how you say, the Luxembourg Gardens."

"How do I find Houdini?"

All the cats went silent. Keri didn't know if she should ask another question or not. She was about to inquire how long the flight took when a small white cat (no bigger than Sally) jumped off a tall stack of luggage and sauntered right up to her feet. He had three black splotches on his back, and a yellowish brown face with intense blue eyes. "I'm Houdini," he said. "What do you want to know?"

"Oh . . . well, Mr. Houdini . . . First of all, is Madeleine okay?"

"For now she is. But who knows if she gets mixed up with Félon."

"Is it true that he's going to fight Madeleine's brother Jules?"

"That's what everyone says."

"Do you know when?"

"Word is, tomorrow at dusk."

"Where?"

"If I knew that, I'd be a rich cat. Everyone wants to see that fight."

"But why does Jules want to fight him?"

"L'amour," Charlotte piped in, *"pour une femme."*

"I don't understand."

"Amore," explained Puccini. "He's in love."

"With who?"

"That no-good tramp Mimi Malone." Houdini went on to tell Keri and Sally about Félon's ex-girlfriend from the Bronx. Mimi was notorious for getting male cats to fawn all over her, and even to bring her live mice at her slightest whim. Once, a perfectly rational cat named Pierre had jumped into the Seine River and tried to swim across, just to prove how much he loved her. He drowned, of course. Mimi ran straight to the Champs-Élysées and bragged that she had every cat in Paris wrapped around her little paw. "She can dance. I'll grant you that," said Houdini. "But I'd rather throw myself off the Eiffel Tower than get mixed up with a dame like her."

"She told Jules that if he didn't fight Félon, she would never be seen near Montmartre with him again," gossiped Charlotte. "Who does she think she is?"

"Now, I do not know this for a fact," said Puccini, "but a friend of mine who knows Mimi personally told me that she once had a litter of five kittens, and—"

"*Mon Dieu*, don't tell her that," Charlotte interrupted. "*Quelle tragédie!*"

"Tell me what?"

"One day," Puccini continued, "Mimi decided that she was sick and tired of the demands of motherhood. So she led all her kittens to the Pont de Tournelle to teach them a new dance. One by one they *jetéed* off the bridge and into the river. She *claimed* that had they confused their left paw with their right, which I myself do not entirely believe."

"What happened?"

"They drowned," Charlotte said spitefully. "Mimi ran to the top of the bell tower of Notre Dame and cried out, "*Mes enfants*, all my babies are drowned."

This story really upset Keri, and Sally, too, for that matter. "How could a mother do that to her own babies?" Keri asked.

"That's Mimi Malone," said Houdini. "I warned Madeleine to stay away from the likes of her."

"I'm starving," Sally blurted out of nowhere.

"You're hungry, no problem. These bags are full of food. Puccini!" Houdini called. "What do we have to eat?"

For the rest of the flight, Keri and the twenty-eight cats (including Sally) feasted on chips, sausages, cheese, even a large bag of M&M's. "Why anyone would want to bring food to Paris is beyond me," Charlotte said, rolling her eyes.

Meanwhile, Houdini entertained the party with stories about Psyche, the mother of Madeleine and Jules. "I first saw her when I was a young tom living on the docks of Newburyport. I'm originally from Columbus, Ohio, see, but my family—my human family—moved around a lot. Psyche was an actress, maybe the greatest who ever lived. I was lucky enough to be in the audience when she played Alice's cat, in you know, *Through the Looking Glass*. Psyche had an exquisite face, like Madeleine, but she was pure white. What a performer, I'll tell you. She could make you laugh, cry, whatever, with a turn of her head. She had grace, emotion, looks . . . She had it all."

Houdini gazed wistfully over the heaps of luggage. "I loved her the moment I laid eyes on her. Once, I found a play program some human had left on the grass. Her picture was there on the cover: white hair, green eyes, glowing fangs . . . What can I say? I grabbed it and went backstage. 'Miss Psyche,' I said, 'could I please have your paw print?' She gave it to me, too. They just don't make 'em any better than her. So I stuck around for a while—never missed a performance. The humans started calling me the Cheshire Cat. 'Hey,' I said, 'My name's Houdini—*Houdini*.' Did they listen? No. But they fed me every night, so who cares? Right? All and all, I'd say it was the best time in my life. Then the show closed and Psyche was gone. And me? I disappeared, no good-bye, nothing. 'Cause that's what I do. The next summer, I went to see *Puss in Boots,* figuring she'd be Puss. Sure, it's a guy's part, but with the right costume and makeup, she could pull it off. But instead, they cast a human in the role. I don't know, he could move well for . . . you know . . . one of them. No offense, but it's kind of hard to . . . what's the phrase . . . suspend disbelief. You know what I mean? Well, she was something else. My pal Frankie said she moved to Minneapolis. Never heard another word about her, but I still think of her. So when I learned that Jules got in a scrape with Félon, and that Madeleine was looking for him, I just had to . . . you know . . . see what I could do—for Psyche's sake."

"I bet my Aunt Wendy knows what happened to Psyche," Keri offered. "She lives with Madeleine."

"I would love to see that cat again."

After that, Keri asked the baggage cats questions about their many travels. She learned that Egypt was the favored destination of almost every cat. All of them had seen the Pyramids, and a dozen or more claimed to have ties to ancient Egyptian felines. "Mimi swears that she was once Cleopatra in a former life," Charlotte snickered. Then all the cats started badmouthing Mimi, so much so that Keri began to feel sorry for her.

After one solid hour of the cattiest talk Keri had ever heard, she finally tried to change the subject. "Do any of you like the saxophone?" she asked. Well, that was all it took. Once Keri pulled out her sax, there was no more talk of Mimi Malone—or anything else, for that matter. Those cats sang and danced around the baggage compartment for hours. Before they knew it, their plane had landed at Charles de Gaulle Airport.

Now they had to find a way off the plane. *And then what?* Just as Keri began to panic, the latch of the baggage compartment sprang open. "What if they see us?" she whispered to Houdini.

"Hang tight, and when I give the signal, follow me." Houdini waited until the French baggage handlers took their first cigarette break, and then he slinked off the plane. He led Keri and the cats all the way around the east side of the airport. Keri ran quickly, ducking now and again to avoid detection. Her heart raced as her feet pounded the pavement, then grass, then more pavement. At last they arrived at what looked like an abandoned taxi stand.

Do taxis even stop here? Keri wondered as she examined the crumbling concrete and broken signs around them. She picked Sally up and held her tight. For nearly an hour, they stayed there. Maybe they were exhausted from dancing, or maybe a breeze of uncertainty began to penetrate their thoughts, but no one said a word. In the silence, Keri thought about her mom and dad. She needed to call them as soon as she found a phone. She thought about Dan. Would he be asleep? What time was it anyway? She thought about a lot of things. But Keri never imagined that she and Sally were about to embark on the most exciting, and the most dangerous, part of their adventure.

7

Keri Tarr at the Luxembourg Gardens

With the help of Houdini, Keri and Sally found an Algerian taxi driver who drove them to Michèle's apartment free of charge. It was eight forty-five in the morning when the driver dropped them off at a tiny brick alleyway called le passage du Montenegro. Michèle was surprised to find her friend's niece sitting on her doorstep when she returned from the bakery. She invited Keri and Sally up to her apartment, but explained that she was late for work. "Take these keys," she said, "so you can let yourself in and out. Oh, and eat whatever you want. I'll be back around six."

After thanking her host, Keri asked Michèle if she could please change thirty-two dollars into French money. Michèle counted out two hundred and fifty francs, and suggested that Keri use the phone to call her aunt. "Dial 001, the area code, and then the number. There are maps of Paris and guidebooks on that shelf. I think some are in English. *Au revoir.*"

"Do you know a cat named Mimi Malone?" Keri called out.

"No, I don't think so."

"We think Jules might be with her. But don't worry, we'll find him."

"That would be a good thing. *Bonne chance,*" said Michèle as she grabbed her raincoat and umbrella and headed out the door, "good luck." And she ran down the spiral staircase and out to the alleyway.

Keri looked at the phone. "Let's see, it's nine o'clock here, and it's six hours earlier in Boston. That means it's three o'clock in the morning there. It's early, but I think we'd better call." First Keri tried her house, but there was no answer. "That's weird. Nobody's home." She didn't know that Dan and her parents were camped out at Aunt Wendy's apartment, hoping to hear back from the police. When she tried to call Aunt Wendy, her aunt's voicemail picked up after only one ring. "I should leave a message," she decided. "Hi, this is Keri. Sally and me are in Paris. Michèle said I could use her phone. We're going to go find Madeleine and Jules now. I'll try to call you later. Don't worry." Unfortunately, the police had dialed Aunt Wendy's number moments before Keri did to say that the missing girl's bike had been spotted in a driveway on Chestnut Street. Keri's dad had instructed the police to call the moment they found out anything. But as a result, the family missed Keri's call, and Aunt Wendy didn't think to check her messages until nine o'clock that morning. By then Keri was gone.

Michèle's apartment was full of books. Most of them were in French, but Keri saw *A Tale of Two Cities* and *Frankenstein* in English. The walls were covered with interesting artwork and photographs. "Look, Sally!" she exclaimed. Theater posters for *Cinderella* and *Peter Pan in Kensington Gardens* were plastered to the kitchen cabinets. "The Children's Theatre of Newburyport," Keri read. "Wow! I wonder if Psyche was in those plays?"

Keri found a street map, a guidebook called *Frommer's Paris,* a small French phrase book, and a map of le Metro. She remembered seeing a Metro sign for Telegraphe before the taxi turned the corner onto Michèle's street. Keri searched the map and located a stop on the Brown Line called Telegraphe.

"Terrific," said Sally. "Now we know where we are. But where are we going?"

Keri wasn't sure. "Charlotte said that Houdini found Madeleine in some garden. What did she call it? Les Jardins . . . the Luxembourg Gardens." Keri found les Jardins du Luxembourg in the guidebook and discovered that Odéon was the closest Metro stop. "Let's start there." She made a couple of tuna sandwiches from ingredients she found in the fridge, wrapped them up, and stuffed them, and Michèle's books, into her saxophone case. Then she and Sally headed to the Metro. As they approached the station, Keri glanced up at the sky. *It looks pretty clear,* she thought.

The Paris Metro was intimidating. The escalator from the street was so steep that Sally had to bury her face in Keri's neck until they reached the bottom. "How do I get a ticket?" Keri asked herself. She looked through Michèle's phrase book, and then the guidebook. "Okay, I can do this." She walked up to the ticket booth, passed a twenty franc note under the glass and said (very slowly), *"Un billet pour le*

Metro, s'il vous plait." The ticket taker shoved a blue ticket and some coins back. *"Merci,"* Keri said.

Keri stared at the huge Metro map in the station. "This is harder than Boston," she sighed. "Let's see. We have to take the brown line and go ten stops to Châtelet. Then we switch to this dark pink line and go three stops to Odéon. And we're there." Sally was completely confused. "Don't worry," Keri told her.

On the train, Keri read to Sally from the guidebook. "'Marie de Médici, the much-neglected wife of Henry IV, ordered the Palais du Luxembourg built in 1612. She planned to live there with her 'witch' friend, Leonora. The queen didn't get to enjoy her palace for very long. She was forced into exile by her son, Louis XIII, after he discovered that she was plotting to overthrow him.'"

"Gee," added Keri, "I wonder if the witch still lives there?"

"Who cares?" said Sally. "Is it lunchtime yet?"

"No."

"Just thought I'd ask."

After changing trains and stopping to ask several friendly-looking Parisians for directions, Keri and Sally rode the escalator up to the street at Odéon. Once outside, Keri looked up anxiously as dark clouds began to fill the sky. "Sally, we have to find Madeleine soon." By studying the map, Keri discovered that they had crossed the River Seine to the Left Bank of Paris. The rue de l'Odéon brought them past the Luxembourg Palace to the Gardens, where a brightly colored advertisement for a marionette theatre captured her attention. *That would be fun,* she thought. But there was no time for amusements. Keri and Sally were greeted at the garden gate by a fierce beast with open jaws, painted to look like an ancient mosaic. Under the creature were written the words PAS CHIEN. "No Dogs," Keri translated from her book. Sally liked that rule.

Keri roamed through the rows and row of hedges, searching for some sign of Madeleine. Finally they came to a large water basin in the center of the garden and sat down to rest under the statue of Geneviève, the patron saint of Paris. Keri was impressed by the saint's long sculpted pigtails, which reached all the way down to her thighs. "Now what?" Sally asked as they stared into the glistening pool of water.

"At least it's not raining," Keri said, trying to put a positive light on things. But the moment she spoke those words, raindrops began bouncing off the basin water. "Oh no!" Keri grabbed Sally and glanced around for shelter. She saw a blue awning at the far side of the park and was about to make a dash for it when she heard a strange voice behind her.

"Pssst, Keri Tarr. *Suivez-moi.*" Before she could find the French words in her book, the small calico cat took off down the path. Keri ran after him as he darted through a maze of hedges and elm trees, across the street, and down several alleyways that led to the Seine River.

"Where are we going?" Keri called out. By now it was starting to pour.

"Suivez-moi," the speckled cat repeated, and then scurried down the quai Saint-Bernard. Keri followed him across one bridge to the Ile Saint-Louis, and then over another back to

the Right Bank of Paris. She was out of breath, but the myste-
rious cat was her only lead. She chased him down the avenue
de l'Opera and across the boulevard des Capucines, where he
finally stopped behind the Palais de Garnier.

"Voilà," said their guide.

Keri tried to read the sign above the door: PORTE DE
L'ESTRADE. Then she knocked, but no one answered.

"Allez," said the drenched cat impatiently. The sky exploded in thunder.

"Try the door knob," Sally pleaded.

Luckily, the door was unlocked, so Keri and the two cats slipped inside. After wringing as much water as she could from her skirt, Keri pulled out her phrase book. *"Porte de l'Estrade* . . . stage door." She didn't realize it, but they were standing backstage at the Palais de la Danse, home to the most celebrated dance troupes in Europe.

"Suivez-moi," the cat said again, shaking off the rain.

This time Keri had her book in hand. *"Suivez-moi,"* she repeated, thumbing through the pages. "It means . . . follow me." Keri started to laugh, but the speckled cat disappeared down a long spiral staircase that descended six flights to the basement of the palace. They had come too far already to stop now. Keri picked up Sally and made her way down the dark stairway. At the bottom of the stairs, Keri followed the cat through a series of cavernous tunnels and into a large room that echoed with her footsteps.

In the center of the room, a smoky brown cat pranced across a worn-out Persian rug. "It's about time you got here," said the feline with a flash of her fiery yellow eyes. "I'm Mimi Malone."

8

Mimi's escape

From the moment that Aunt Wendy listened to Keri's message, the disappearance of Keri Tarr became an international incident. Government agencies on both sides of the Atlantic scrambled to explain how a ten-year-old girl and her cat had slipped into France undetected. To make matters worse, the taxi driver who had driven Keri to the airport was nowhere to be found.

"How could you have let her go to France?!" exclaimed Keri's dad.

Aunt Wendy tried to explain that although Keri had asked Michèle for her address, she had no idea that her niece would actually go to Paris. "I'm so sorry," cried Aunt Wendy, "I really thought she'd be right back."

Keri's mom, on the other hand, was too upset to say anything. Dan tried to comfort everyone by reminding them that his sister was very resourceful. "She'll be okay. Don't . . ." Even he couldn't finish that sentence. Soon all the local TV stations were airing Keri and Sally's picture. Channel Five provided up-to-the-minute coverage on "The Disappearance of Keri Tarr." In cities and towns across New England, Girl

Scout troops held vigils to pray for Keri's safe return.

"Fritzy," called Mrs. Taylor from her living room sofa, "isn't that the nice girl who came over on Christmas Day with her cat?" Fritzy took one look at the photo of Sally on the television and ran out of the house.

When Michèle returned from work that evening, she was greeted by Lieutenant Colbert of the French police, Mrs. Hilton from the American Embassy, and a dozen or so newspaper reporters who were assigned to the case. Her apartment had been ransacked by two police officers looking for clues, so Michèle was not in a very pleasant mood. Still, she tried to help the lieutenant as much as she could. She told him that a few maps and guidebooks were missing and some tuna fish and bread. Oh yes, and Keri had mentioned something about a cat named Mimi. But none of this information seemed to interest the officer in the least.

Meanwhile Keri, Sally, Mimi, and the black-and-white cat (whose name turned out to be Moucheté) sat on the purple Persian carpet in the basement of the palace and picnicked on tuna fish sandwiches. They were surrounded by broken tubas, loosely strung cellos, rusty cymbals, and half a dozen other musical instruments that lay about the room covered in dust. Keri was glad that her saxophone was safely tucked away in its case. Sounds of dancers rehearsing and musicians tuning their instruments echoed down through the heating vent from the theater six flights above. Keri listened as the choreographer counted out the rhythm, her high-pitched voice reverberating throughout the room.

"Usually, I do not eat this much," said Mimi as she devoured half the tuna that Keri had set aside for Moucheté. "I am trying to keep my figure. I think that is so important when you are in the public eye. The demands on us celebrities are tremendous. You have no idea of the sacrifices I've made."

Keri kept trying to bring the conversation back to Jules and Félon, but Mimi seemed disposed to talk only about herself. "Yes," Keri would say, "but can we stick to the subject?"

"Alas, it is too difficult for me to think about my poor Jules fighting that bully."

At one point, Keri got up the courage to ask Mimi about her kittens—the ones who had danced off the bridge. She couldn't get that image out of her mind.

"My career has always kept me from pursuing the joys of motherhood," Mimi replied. Keri wasn't sure what to make of that answer.

"Look," she finally said, "*you* sent Moucheté to bring *us* here. We have a lot of work to do. So if you're not going to cooperate, then Sally and I are leaving."

"Who said I would not cooperate? I am entirely at your disposal."

"Good. Then, did you tell Jules that if he didn't fight that Félon cat, you would break up with him?"

"That is entirely false. I bet you heard that from that no-good blabbermouth Charlotte. When you have risen to the top like I have, Keri, there is always someone below who wants to tear you down."

"Were you ever Félon's girlfriend?"

"Yeah, Artie and I used to be an item."

"Are you still seeing him?"

"I am not. Artie got too weird for me. All those skulls and bones started giving me the creeps. See, at the beginning, it was all romance. Sure, I knew he had his problems, but he had good points, too. For one, he is a great dancer. The two of us used to go out every night. Jazz clubs, parties, you name it. We would dance till our paws ached. The envy of Paris, that's what we was."

"What happened?"

"Well, when he moved his place of residence from the trash can in Montmartre to the caves of the Catacombs, it all started to go downhill."

Mimi explained how Artie (as she called Félon) was obsessed with all the skeletons that were displayed in the underground caverns. Keri looked up the Catacombs in her guidebook. She read that in 1785, Paris officials had moved some six million skeletons from overcrowded cemeteries into the thousand yards of tunnels that had been once used as quarries during the Middle Ages. At first, Mimi found Artie's new digs exciting. They'd invite the most notorious cats in the city to Tango among the skulls and bones. But after a while, she decided that there was more to life than death, so she escaped.

"Artie," Mimi said, licking the last bit of tuna from the side of her mouth, "was the possessive type. He once told me that if I ever left him, he would kill me. I believed him, too. So I ran all the way to the northeast of Paris and hid out in the passage du Montenegro. That is where I met Jules. Apparently, the big lug had been watching me for days, dazzled by my beauty. Finally he gets the nerve to speak to me. He says, '*Pardonnez-moi, mademoiselle,* could I interest you in some leftover rinds of Brie?' Just like that. Now, he is a gentleman, I mean, he really knows how to treat a lady like myself. Well, he is no dancer, but what the heck, he was a nice guy."

"One day, we was chasing mice on the *Champs-Elysées*, when who do we run into but Artie. He was prowling the avenue scaring tourists into dropping their Häagen-Dazs. I wanted to run. But he took one look at me and pounced. There I was, my neck pinned to the pavement, his fangs piercing my skin. I tried to break free, but he was too strong. I thought one of my lives was over for sure. Then, whack! Jules was on top of us scratching and biting. I never seen nothing like it. It was like he was possessed or something. By the time Jules was done, half of Artie's left ear was gone and the big creep was whimpering like a kitten. So then Jules says, 'If you touch one patch of fur on Mimi again, Monsieur Félon, you'll have to answer to me!' And we started to walk away. But Artie mustered all his strength and let out a howl that could be heard clear to the Louvre. Within seconds, a hundred of the most sinister cats in Paris surrounded us. I thought they was going to kill us right there and then. Then Artie stalks up to Jules and says, 'Okay, big shot. You think you're tough. Let's see how tough you really are.' And then he challenges him to a duel in the Catacombs. With all those cats watching, poor

Jules couldn't say no. He agrees to meet Artie a week from then, which is tonight."

"Where's Jules now?" Keri asked.

"'That is the worst part. Artie did not trust Jules to show up for the fight. So the next day he had his thugs grab him, and they hauled him off to the Catacombs, where he is currently being held, poor guy. Meanwhile, Artie's been working out day and night gettin' ready for the big fight."

Keri asked Mimi if she knew anything about Madeleine. "I heard Jules's sister came to Paris. But I have not had the pleasure of making her acquaintance."

"How do we get to the Catacombs?"

Mimi and her sidekick Moucheté led Keri and Sally back up to the avenue de l'Opera. By then the rain had stopped. The Catacombs were too far away to walk, so Keri pulled the map of the Metro from her saxophone case. But before she could locate the nearest station, Mimi stopped five taxis by walking out onto the rue de Casanova (causing a minor traffic accident in the process). They loaded into the only cab that managed to avoid the pileup.

"Bonjour, Mimi," said the elderly driver as he tipped his hat to her.

"Hey François, would ya take us to the Prison de Conciergerie?"

"Bien sûr."

"What about the Catacombs?" Keri protested.

"Just a little detour. You may not know this, but I was once Marie Antoinette—in a former life. I must pause to mourn the deaths of my fellow aristocrats who were beheaded during the French Revolution. My cell is still there, exactly as I left it, before . . . you know . . ." Mimi made a gesture with her paw across her throat. "I'll tell you, it was a terrible time to be a queen."

As they passed the prison, Keri instructed the driver to take them to the Catacombs. Looking out the window, she watched as the sun was beginning to set over the throngs of cars trying to leave Paris during rush hour. She worried that they might be too late. And what would she do when they arrived?

"Look, Keri," Sally interrupted, "we don't even know if Madeleine will be there. Why don't we go back to Michèle's and have a nice dinner . . ."

"Sally, we have to stop this fight."

"How?"

Keri was silent.

9

Artaud Félon and the Empire of the Dead

As the taxi carrying Keri and her company of cats arrived at the Catacombs, her parents, brother, and aunt were circling Charles de Gaulle Airport in a Boeing 727, preparing to land in Paris. The pilot had been briefed on the situation and was instructed to inform the family of any updates from the ground. But none came. At the airport, the family was bombarded by throngs of reporters who wanted to know everything from what Keri was wearing to when she had first spoken with cats. A rumor had even circulated that Keri was hired by the wife of the French president to find her missing cat. But no one at the *Palais de l'Élysée* could be reached for comment. Recent photos of Keri were distributed to the press, and soon her face was broadcast on every major news channel.

All eyes were focused on Keri's family, which is probably why no one noticed twenty-five baggage cats scampering out of the plane's luggage compartment and into a taxi. In fact, over one thousand baggage cats flew into Charles de Gaulle Airport that evening, more than ten times the usual number.

But Lieutenant Colbert and the police couldn't be bothered with a few stray cats; they had a missing girl on their hands. The detective escorted the family through a sea of flashing cameras, and then to Michèle's apartment, where they anxiously waited for Keri's return.

Meanwhile, in the dank tunnels of the Catacombs, Artie and his gang of thugs prepared for the duel. Eight cats had been kidnapped and forced to fight Félon, just for practice. Later their bodies were found floating in the Seine River. Now Artie was ready. The thought of tearing Jules to shreds made him smirk with anticipation. "Can we go get him, boss?" snarled a brown-and-black striped alley cat named Griffe.

"Bring him to me. I'll rip both his ears off, just for starters."

Locked away in a tiny cavern, Jules paced back and forth across the heaps of crushed skulls and bones that were strewn about the ground. He was a pitiful sight—half starved and covered with scratches and welts. *Everything happened so quickly,* he thought as he dodged the drips and drops of water that leaked from the roof of the cave. One moment, he and Mimi had been joyously chasing mice. The next instant, he was being dragged by the neck over miles of jagged cobblestones, and then wham, thrown into the most morbid prison imaginable. Now he doubted that he'd ever see Mimi again. Most of all, he longed to curl up on Michèle's lap by the fire.

Outside the Catacombs, Keri tried to pay the taxi driver fifty francs.

"Non, non, non. C'est Mimi."

"Thanks, François. You're a doll." Mimi blew him a kiss.

"*Je t'aime, Mimi.*"

"Oh, you too, hon."

Keri thanked the elderly cabbie, and the taxi sped away. The street was deserted, cold, and gray. Through the fog, Keri could see an ancient stone building. Sally jumped into Keri's arms and nestled on her shoulder. As they walked towards the entrance, Keri noticed a large sign posted on the door that read: LE MUSÉE EST FERMÉ with a red diagonal line across it. "It's closed," she sighed. "How do we get in?"

"No problem." Mimi led Keri and the others quickly down a tiny alleyway that ran alongside and then in back of the museum. The dark mist that hovered over them sent chills up Keri's spine, and she hugged Sally tight.

"Where are we going, Mimi?" No reply. Finally, Mimi reached her destination: a manhole cover wedged open wide enough for her and Moucheté to slip through. "Wait," Keri pleaded as she pushed the metal disk out of her way and descended into the sewer pipe. The water in the pipe came up to Keri's ankles, and it splashed over her face and skirt as she followed the two cats through a maze of tunnels.

Finally, they came to an ancient metal gate. Half of the spikes had rusted away, but Keri could still make out the skull and crossbones that adorned the center pole. "What is this place?" she asked, covering her nose to avoid the stench.

"Tourists call it the Catacombs, but to Artie and me, it will always be the Empire of the Dead."

The rusted gate had not been used by humans since 1830, when the chief of police had ordered the entrance sealed from

the public. Keri took off her saxophone case and slipped it (and Sally) under the gate. The stone floor was covered in grime. She lay down as flat as she could and maneuvered her body around the sharp spikes and through the entrance. "Keri," Sally whimpered, "I don't think we should be in here."

Keri stroked Sally's head and tried to calm her. "Don't be scared. It will be okay." But Keri couldn't even convince herself of that.

By the time Keri reached the inner sanctum of the Catacombs, Jules had been dragged out of his cell and down several corridors to the Passion Crypt, where Félon anxiously awaited his prey. Every alley cat in Paris was there, hundreds of despicable creatures who were particularly attracted to the smell of death. From behind the Rotunda de Tobias (a barrel shaped pillar made entirely of bones), Keri heard them screeching and wailing. She peeked out to see Jules being hauled before Félon. He could barely stand. "In this corner," Griffe announced, "is the meanest, toughest, most powerful cat in all of France: Artaud Félon." The rabblement hooted and cheered. "And in this corner is a lowly, good-for-nothing coward who will soon be food for the fishes." Hisses and jeers reverberated though the cave.

From the corner of her eye, Keri caught a glimpse of a small cat with three black splotches on his back and a yellowish brown face. He was perched on a ledge high above the other cats. "It's Houdini," she whispered. Beside him, filled with terror, was none other than Madeleine.

"Let's grab your aunt's cat and get out of here," Sally pleaded.

"So without further ado," Griffe continued, "let the battle begin!"

Keri watched as Madeleine stood poised to jump into the fray. She had to do something. "Not so fast," Keri shouted as she strutted between Félon and Jules. "This is not a fair fight."

"Get the human out of here!" the alley cats sneered.

"I'm not leaving without Jules." She picked up the shivering cat and cradled him in her arms. She was about to turn and walk out when two alley cats pounced on Sally and clutched her neck in their fangs.

"Leave her alone," Keri protested.

"You want your cat back," Artie scoffed, "then put Jules down and clear out."

This was too much. What could she do? Tears started to roll down her cheeks as Keri watched Sally squirming beneath two ferocious cats. "Stop it," she cried, but they kept on biting and scratching. Suddenly, an enormous orange-and-white cat came barreling out from one of the caverns and jumped full force on Sally's attackers.

"Fritzy?!" Sally shouted.

That was it. Behind Fritzy were over a thousand baggage cats who had made their way to Paris to help Madeleine. Houdini had spread the word on both sides of the Atlantic. In Boston, Max and Joe had worked around the clock to bring volunteers to Logan Airport. Even Beau and the Soderberg cats were there. Now it was the baggage cats against the alley cats. Keri held fast to Sally as Artie's goons wrapped their tails around trash can lids and smashed the heads of their opponents. "That's not fair!" she shouted.

The baggage cats fought back. "Go Ivan!" Sally cheered as the Russian blue zippered Griffe, and eight other alley cats, inside a nylon carry-on bag with his teeth. "Oh no!" Keri gasped. A gang of alley cats had pinned Houdini to the cave wall, and Félon was about to strike him with a trash can lid. Keri rushed to save him, but suddenly Houdini vanished into thin air.

"Now where did Madeleine go?" Keri had managed to hold on to Jules and Sally, but in all the commotion, she lost sight of her aunt's cat.

"Please can we just go," Sally begged her. Keri searched frantically though the myriad battling cats for Jules' sister, her arms bleeding from scratches and bites. She was surrounded by hordes of vicious beasts who were prepared to fight to the death. Covering her face, Keri managed to cross through the mayhem and back to the pillar. Now Mimi and Moucheté were gone, too. "Madeleine!" Keri shouted over the ocean of bloodied cats. *It's hopeless,* she thought, and she slid down the side of the pillar exhausted.

"*Ciao,* Keri Tarr. You have to stop all this fighting."

Keri turned around and saw a dapper tabby with a white patch on his nose. "Oh, Puccini," she replied, "it's you. What am I going to do?"

"*La musica.*"

"What?"

"Play your saxophone."

"Why?"

"Just do it."

Keri realized that she was sitting right on top of her saxophone case. She carefully pulled the instrument out and placed it to her lips. "What should I play?"

"Well, you know, cats are slaves to jazz."

Keri played the loudest, jazziest tune she could think of. Within seconds, every cat in the place stopped fighting. Cats who were ripping and clawing each other apart one moment were suddenly dancing with abandon the next. Alley cats began dancing with baggage cats. Keri strolled through the battlefield-turned-dance floor belting out her song. The notes hypnotized her audience.

In the center of the room, Mimi and Artie pranced and frolicked. Sally was so entranced that she shimmied right up to Fritzy and they started to swing. Up on the ledge, Keri spotted Madeleine dancing with Houdini. He swung her to and fro until she was dizzy. Keri carefully made her way through the crowd and under the ledge. "Madeleine," she called quickly, then continued to play.

This interruption caught Houdini off balance. He lost hold of Madeleine's paw, sending her flying off the stone ridge. Keri dropped her saxophone just in time to catch her. But as soon as the music stopped, the cats ceased their dancing and glared at their partners. Before they could pounce on each other, Keri picked up her instrument and continued playing. *That was a close one,* she thought. She gathered up Sally, Jules, Madeleine, and Fritzy and headed down the tunnel playing as loud as she could. When Keri reached the gate, she shoved the cats between the spikes. She stopped playing long enough to get herself and the saxophone out, then belted out one final riff before running down the sewer pipes and up through the manhole.

Inside the crypt, the alley cats and the baggage cats awoke from their musical spell. They looked around dumbfounded. "*Mon Dieu,* where did they go?" Artie hissed.

"I dunno," answered Griffe.

Artie noticed for the first time that the alley cats were outnumbered.

"Hey, boss, what do we do?"

Now all eyes were on Artie. He strutted to the center of the crypt and raised his paw. "My opponent, a yellow-bellied coward, has sunk so low as to bring in a human to save him. *Donc,* I have no other choice but to call off this fight." The alley cats booed. "*Silence!* This is not over. *Non,* I will find Jules. And when I do, I will kill him over and over again until every one of his lives is used up. *Comprenez-vous?* Jules has not seen the last of me. And neither has that Keri Tarr. I make this promise to you." A few seconds later, Artie and his thugs were gone.

When Keri and the cats reached the street, they were blinded by a whirling glare of lights. Apparently, the silver-haired cabbie who had driven Keri to the Catacombs had recognized her picture on TV and called the station. Now over fifty patrol cars flashed their lights outside the museum entrance. News and television reporters from around the globe shouted questions at the famous Cat Detective: "Are you the real Keri Tarr?" "Did you solve your case?" "Did you find Madeleine?"

"Keri!" her mom screamed, pushing her way through the crowd.

"Mom!" Keri hugged her mother.

Before they could say another word, a *New York Times* reporter interrupted their reunion. "Keri, viewers around the world have been following your story. Can you tell us what happened?"

"I found my aunt's cat."

"How did you know where she was?"

"That's my job."

"Can you tell us how you got to Paris?"

"I'm sorry, I can't."

"So, what's next for the Cat Detective?"

After half an hour of ceaseless questions and photos, Keri just wanted to go home.

For the next twenty-four hours, families from Bolton to Moscow watched video clips of *"La Délivrance de Keri Tarr,"* as Lieutenant Colbert referred to the incident. Pictures of Keri holding Sally, Aunt Wendy hugging Madeleine, and Michèle petting Jules were played and replayed throughout the following day. In New England, local stations even displayed a split screen of Keri holding Fritzy in Paris and Mrs. Taylor waving to her cat from her living room in Bolton. That night, Mrs. Hilton of the American Embassy invited the Tarrs to stay at the elegant Hôtel Elysa-Luxembourg, near the gardens where Keri had begun her search. They were escorted to the presidential suite and served a late-night snack of salmon in honor of Sally.

The family caught an early-afternoon flight back to Boston the next day. At first, airport officials threatened to place Sally, Madeleine, and Fritzy in quarantine, but Lieutenant Colbert convinced them to bend the rules. During the seven-hour flight, Keri and Sally watched movies and listened to music. Smiling flight attendants served them lunch, dinner, and an endless supply of peanuts and other snacks. As she gazed out the window, Keri couldn't help but wonder if Houdini or any of the other baggage cats were stowed away in the luggage compartment below. "Sally, will we ever see them again?"

"Who cares?" Sally answered, scratching her right ear.

"Fritzy sure was brave."

"I suppose."

"He saved your life."

"Perhaps."

"Maybe I should invite him and Mrs. Taylor over to our house."

"If you want to."

"Do you want me to?"

"I didn't say no." Sally stretched, circled three times around Keri's lap, and then lay down for a nap.

That evening, finally home again, Keri took a long bubble bath and then curled up with Sally and Mew in bed. Her mother, who had been all smiles and hugs since Keri's return, now looked very serious as she tucked in her daughter. "Keri," she said slowly.

"Yeah, Mom."

"You know that your Dad and I are very proud of you for finding Madeleine."

"I know."

"And you also know that we love you very much."

"Yeah."

"But if you ever, ever, ever go off on your own like that . . . "

"I'm sorry."

"You have to promise me that you'll never do it again."

"Don't worry, Mom."

"Promise."

Keri thought for a moment. "But Félon is still out there, and I don't know what happened to Mimi Malone, or Puccini. And if Houdini was in trouble, I might have to . . ."

"All right, all right . . . Just promise that you'll try to be more careful."

"I will." Keri yawned. "Good night, Mom."

"Sleep tight, sweetheart." And she kissed her daughter goodnight.

Keri pulled Sally up close to her, and they fell fast asleep.